Thank You Resiliency, But I Am Tired

Alyshia Bradley

Thank You Resiliency, But I Am Tired

By Alyshia Bradley

Copyright 2019 by Alyshia Bradley

Looking for an explanation.

A re-examination of my thoughts,

Memories

My feelings on me

And my inability to love the right way.

Where do I start?...

In the beginning of September, my grief began to coalesce in my throat and by the 11th day, I let out a scream.

One that every woman recognized.

One that my broken heart would memorize, greet and behave accordingly to.

I found it painfully laughable that my grief could get together just to form that scream, But we could not.

We could not get it together.

"Damn kid, you are about to have a time..." I say that to myself right after every breakup.

 The hardest parts of break ups for me are not the lack of person; but me having to deal with myself.

I am certain to lose my damn mind.

Times like this, man I question "am I worthy?"

Times like this, man I question "am I worthy?"

Times like this, man I question "am I worthy?"

Times like this, man I question "am I worthy?"

Am I deserving?

To be alone now.

I suppose.

It was a really self-obsessed thing to say "the hardest part after a breakup, is dealing with myself and not the lack of person."

But that has been my experience.

People leave and I am left with myself.

So insensitive, self-obsessed, possibly but it is also ownership...I am left to deal with myself.

Heal with myself.

I was mean.

Kind of like that old lady who spits because she spent her "allotted Black Woman woes".

I didn't want to be bothered.

Everybody knows.

I feel like I should thank you for making me address my anger.

I did not expect it to replace you. I did not expect for you to haunt me. I did not expect for you to hate me. I expected my every give-in to grief.

Grief, at least, holds me tight. Consistently.

I try to grieve as quiet as possible.

Disappear.

It is embarrassing.

This one especially...an ended engagement.

I had just tried on dresses.

So no, you won't get the whole story on how I am doing, the breakup, whose fault it is, what I'm doing now or where I'm going...I am quiet in that regard.

I try to grieve as quietly as possible, save for a few people. A team. I get needy and moody and everything worries me, and I can't trust myself being as quiet as possible.

In my actions, my actions are loud as hell. You can see the breakup in my walk, my actions, the stupid cringe worthy things that do come out of my mouth when I speak... I try to stay quiet. I try.

But we know what it means when a child is alone and quiet for too long…

Don't Go Looking In A Ladies Purse

 The contents of my purse are as follows: 2 different kinds of Chapstick, a half-smoked j, and a whole lotta truth. It makes it hard to swallow.

 The contents of my purse are as follows: my organizer, 22 cents, and a copy of 'Mercury is in Retrograde but The Rent is Still Due'. That shit is still due.

 The contents of my purse are as follows: A little bit of today's, yesterday's, and tomorrow's.

 The contents of my purse are as follows: Those "always losing them" Bobby pins, A book on how to make amends, Some Washington's but no Benjamin's.

 And a whole lot of old woes. Kept to myself so no one knows.

My mom says that a lady is entitled to a few secrets.

I have a few, I don't like to keep many because to me, secrets lead to shame and guilt and those are powerful things.

They've already destroyed me once, so the scariness that can come with secrets does not bother me...the judgement is more damning though. In my most anxious moments I feel the whispers about me, the "poor things", the unsolicited opinions or sides taken.

They slink into my ears, egged on by my anxiety about my future alone and bombarded by screams from past failed relationships. Damn kid, you're going to have a time...because you fail to learn. That's worse than secrets. That's worse than being without you. That is worse than being alone. I fail to learn.

In now 'My Room':

I am haunted by things that once were, things that were supposed to be.

You are absolutely everywhere and that terrifies me into vulnerability.

Like smilin' at old jokes and chokin' on 'I miss you' through so many angry aka 'I miss you too' tears.

Yeah, I'm grievin', that's what my every action reaction is screamin. All the while I'm thinkin' I'm alive n strivin' survivin' when really, I'm back to six-year-old me sobbin', holdin' a popped balloon.

Shook.

Startled.

Back in The Valley too soon.

This is why it is a bad idea cohabitate with boyfriends.

Cue second mega cleansing, reorganizing and sageing.

It was important for me to reclaim space, make it feel more "me" less "us" just like in every other part of life.

Me and not us fixing this mess that has been made.

I would say mess you made but...what good would blame do at this point?

The hardest part about all of this is the transparency. But I promised me...

When love is tested by true sacrifice, I don't know what it looks like, so my heart and mind don't think twice about convincing myself I don't need it.

I don't deserve it. I don't believe it.

It became an attack on my person, my art, my woman, my pain, my rained-on garments with tears from my heart.

You know, that one hurt garment every hurt person wears after they've been hurt, just to show the world how hurt they've been, all the while trying not to hurt him and him and him.

My patience wearing thin, and that's not good! Cuz that's how you buy love right??? Right?!? I didn't have enough patience to afford your love. Do I have enough change for a sacrifice now? I need to learn how to love the right way Someone please, Show me how. I, the selfish antagonist in many a man's story.

I am not perfect.

A friend of mine tells me one of the biggest problems that plagues our society is fatherlessness... I did not realize how the scarcity of my father in my life affected me so, because not me, I didn't have daddy issues because I knew my dad, I remember thinking that as a kid. You know, you hear the phrase thrown around at school or on TV, "yeah, she's got daddy issues. "some now either very encouraged or very annoyed man will say.

That's what was said about the girl who is a little more than filled out than her gal pals, but it was dangerous when paired with the new interest in boys. That's what was said about the non-trusting or bullshit taking girl who somehow always still had her heartbroken in the cafeteria, that's what was said about the girl who liked sex.

But that was not me, I liked boys but they didn't like me, and I kept my legs closed until seventeen so I couldn't have daddy issues not me, I knew my dad. He was my dad! He wasn't a deadbeat or in jail. He lived in a big beautiful house in Marietta, always drove a Mercedes and I saw him

once or twice a year. Every other
Christmas, sometimes Thanksgiving and
every summer. Not me, no daddy issues
here because I love my dad. He sends me
to camp for a week or two in the summer
and there is always Six Flags or White
Water with my siblings. Not my
dad...because he knows best. He sends the
monthly checks on time. He is a minister
and I trust him and I just wanna be here
in his life...things are cleaner, I have to
squint less to find beauty, people are
happy, there is space, the school, the
church, the' yes darling' phone calls to my
step mom.. I wanted for so long to belong
in my father's upper middle-class world.

 I ached for it. I ached for my father. I
think I still do because I've been
searching for that feeling in the dumbest
places. I wanted to belong in that world,
but I could tell I didn't. I didn't quite
belong to the one back at home either,
which was not horrible but still haunted
with my father's absence. I missed him,
not initially because I don't remember
that part, but when I was old enough to go
visit and leave again i missed him. I know
my brother missed him, and now giving

what I know about love and the situation I bet my mom did too. We were haunted, our faces that looked like his. The fact that we lived where we did. Felt how we felt. Were now privy and exposed to a different kind of lack ...fatherlessness. And that shit stains. This friend of mine with his opinion on fatherlessness just yanked up my rugs, challenged my perspective...has me grieving parts of my life I didn't know I should of.

"En Español.", He said to me. "Necesito un seguriDAD."

You see, he's like a dad except with all the security mine did not come with.
seguriDAD! seguriDAD! The greatest love I've ever had! Except when he failed to explain that I'd be an incomplete mess when he left. Men my demise, my need, my test.
Cuz my seguriDAD would have beaten the lie out of the mouth of the first boy that broke my heart, instead of locking in the untrue gospel of years to come that I am not enough to keep my seguriDAD... I try to be the best 27-year-old daughter you've ever had, really I do, except when I throw myself at men because you weren't there to tell me ladies don't have to act that way.
Cuz mommy said it too but it didn't quite set in. I needed that fatherly touch. Some bass in that voice. I needed a daddy, it wasn't a fair choice and I was so young when it happened I probably didn't even notice his absence.
seguriDAD...seguriDAD... where are you? Are you hiding in the issues that lay dormant in my heart, shaken awake

whenever some other man leaves? I hate you sometimes for sealing my destiny to be confused about love.
Cuz my seguriDAD doesn't protect and serve from birthday cards and visitation once or twice a year.

My seguriDAD wants to hear those troubles melt away in my sobs. Growing up without a father, every little girl gets robbed!

 Effort.

Can you pour that out in make-believe tea? Can you hear it in every missed recital? When you're not with me… Can you braid it into a baby doll's hair? Or write it in a card for me to see? Necesito un seguriDAD para rescatarme.

I ran away.

I wanted to go to my father in Georgia. I remember having conversations with friends all over, inquiring about work conditions, apartment costs, I wanted to flee the area.

I settled for anywhere but home most nights.

Nothing scary, just couch surfing. I was never so angry in my life.

My anger multiplied when at a point I felt he did not take me seriously.

Big no no. He had an attitude of "Oh she will just calm her pretty little head down and come home when she comes to her senses." It plucked a nerve; he could do nothing right after that and I killed in my mind any hope to reconcile. I am certain my behavior surprised and worried my mother. The surprise though was that I could not love him past this. A shame.

In reflection I'm actually sad and ashamed to say I've only been in 1 or 2 relationships that weren't toxic and only 1 of those relationships was I was only the woman...did you catch that? Everything- everyone else made me tired, but that's what happens when you settle for unbalanced love.

That's what happens when you don't know 'a lady's place ' in the grand scheme of things. And that's what happens when you get hurt so much you can't trust...them or yourself... but you feel the need to be everything and everyone else in the world to him but yourself...the woman. Where the fuck did I go? And why do I keep putting myself in small ass boxes for love and acceptance?...

Thank you, resiliency...but I am tired.

Even though this is the worst part...myself...I still miss you too.

I miss the me I was when I was with you, at least the good bits.

I miss who I thought we would be together. I am allowed to be disappointed I didn't get what I wanted or expected.

Truth. No sugar.

I miss dancing in the kitchen with you.
And sharing what was sometimes our
only meal of the day. It was small. But we
were full.

Between drinks and stress smoking cigarettes. Maybe I will have time.

To tell you.

These drinks don't numb shit.

Un-numb:
 That part in the breakup where you start feeling everything and your mind and stomach turn into a swarm of bees. I am feeling every breakup I've ever had because what they've all got in common is me, and my inadequacy. I don't know how to love to be patient, I don't know how to love to be kind. This thought isn't mine it was placed there by my grief, and now I am dying with the belief that I am unlovable.

You think I'm wrong? Well show me evidence, my mind is hell bent in that regard.

I've got years of proof and without a daddy too I shoulda left those damn boys alone knowing damn well I didn't know what to do with them. I hate my skin. You're under it. I hate my sorrow. We funded it. and now I'll dance all night offbeat just like my heart.

 I am bleeding you out, I need a transfusion. What the fuck were we doing?? It was all an illusion. An illusion of what love must be about and now I hate me without a doubt for falling, I've got a contusion and that's how you crawled in and ruined my life! The bees are swarming. The bees are stinging. My heart is bleeding. My ears are ringing. Hearing all the bullshit that made me obese. So please...I am un-numb. I feel all the words you say... please I am un-numb. Say I'll make it through the day.

I used to take inventory of my grieving habits: You didn't eat today...slept longer than normal but not when you should of...you've gotten clumsy lately, forgetful too...sex...a drink...leaning closer to the mirror over the sink cuz, that's the only thing in the vicinity big enough to catch my tears and honestly that's how close I have to get to recognize myself...I stopped taking inventory. I don't recognize myself... Trying to think lighter, prettier thoughts. What am I taking inventory of again??

Memories. Good times. They are too sweet. For sure, they will rot me from the inside.

Please take them. I'm full. I don't want anymore.

Disappointed...but grateful.

I cannot say this next sentence without sounding ungrateful or selfish, so here it is anyway: I never quite get what I want. And that's on me. I settle and then gorge on whatever is provided. I didn't even realize I did that. So, it is me...I'm just a shitty person. So, it is me, I don't know my worth. So, it is me. Well damn...at least now I know.

I've never eaten

 Something as sweet as his lies.

They made me obese.

Something

inside me must have a really strong will to love and be loved.

I love that feeling I get when I'm "done;" that done, done.

That, oh sis is done done.

Oh, you boy bye done.

Oh, you ain't coming back from this done. Yeah...yeah man...we done.

Like Persephone

 I am dragged back to myself

only for a while.

Eventually I get some perspective.

I soothe my expectations, my heart and ego and pick up things that are actually mine.

I am well aware that I am the villain in your story.

That I'll haunt your fractured trust...

That unbalanced love will be your insecurity... I am so sorry.

I take ownership of that.

Does that even matter??

Aren't we all passed along a little broken or tattered?

"Mine" things like: ownership. Once I'm done being angry...and lonely...and horny and all the things I am actually sorry.

Are you listening to me now?

I want to remember this day.

Our daily bread.

Forgive me, I trespassed.

I starved you cuz I was starvin'.

An' I didn't mean no harm an' Will you ever be the same?

I know the time I've had.

I think about yours too, makes me feel sick I did that.

Literally my stomach drops with shame and I know I can't fix it.

You laugh?

Well I laugh too.

How human of me.

How human of you.

You cry?

Well I cry too.

How human of me.

How human of you.

Today God laid me in His palm and told me he will always understand.

He places people to remind me, I am resilient.

I love that I cry with joy.

Being sensitive and an empath is a curse but not when I get a rich, deep understanding of self through poetry.

I've been writing a poem a day for 3 months now.

Some whiney squabbles, some that just make my own heart ache or soar because of the passion in it.

Maybe I should speak poetry all the time.

My mom says I should pray, that way I'm not really alone.

God hears poetry too...

 He calls me, Lovely.

Was I to think that he always found me, Lovely?

Found me under every dark stare.

Every missed button and whine. I whine a lot.

He looked at me a lot, looked for me a lot.

Because, foolish me, I kept forgetting I was found.

I did not see what he saw.

He was like one of those wolves with two different colored eyes, except instead they were black and white.

And he saw me in both instead of just as grey.

It eased my soul.

The ability to live in both eyes just as Lovely. Could I stay there? That's just his eyes. That's just his eyes.

That's just his eyes. And they always find me, Lovely.

The question I've been asking myself lately: Am I done resisting?

Sometimes I think somewhere along the line I became stubborn for the sake of being so and thus resistant to so many things that were most likely good for me...I never wanted to be too girly, but feminine enough to be touched without recoil... Pretty thoughts.

A broken flower

It will grow again with love

So water daily.

My deepest fear is silly really: You know how they say you only have 3 real loves in your life?

Well, I've had all mine, I fear I won't get another.

I just couldn't let them love me... I couldn't let them love me. I need to bend. I need to bend, Before my heart breaks beyond repair.

Time to grow up. And I want to. Wash your worth girl.

Is there someone who stills finds joy in picking up an old penny?

Will smile and dust me off and pocket me?

I'm ready. Could I be considered lucky?

I'm always found on heads so I can look up at the sky and forget the things I dread.

Pick me up.

Note to self:

Stop telling dudes I'm strong as hell.
Because clearly, they cannot handle it.

And neither can I.

 When they decide.

That means So many other things Are
more important than me.

When working on my worth I kind of have to detach from everyone else.

So, if I come off arrogant, and loud like "yikes who hurt that girl..." that's fine. Autonomy is vital.

I felt beautiful

Only once with you looking

 and always without.

 I think I'm starting to hear who I am.

I'm laughing my way to better days; I hope you hear it over everything else. It is intentionally too loud, Intentionally bold and full of joy.

It is all I hear now, I'm on my way to better days, it is my favorite song, My battle cry, My slick clapback. And even my prayer. So, I'm on my way, I can't hear you or anything else.

So feel free to join me, Laugh in harmony.

Baby you are loved

Bathe in that like early joy

Smiling on your face.

I will never fall out of love with myself again.

Amen.

Made in the USA
Middletown, DE
19 December 2019